LAND ABOVE

T0148238

LAND ABOVE

LEIGH CLARKE

 www.trafford.com

North America & international
toll-free: 1 888 232 4444 (USA & Canada)
phone: 250 383 6864 ♦ fax: 812 355 4082

Leigh Clarke

Leigh Clarke received her BFA in Studio Art in 1997, and has taken classes towards a MFA in creative writing. Although she loves to paint, over the past few years she has indulged herself with her writing. Ms. Clarke has also published *This and That*, a book of short stories, and is about to complete the manuscript for Part Two of *Land Above,* which will be entitled, *A New Land*. She is also in the process of writing her memoirs. Ms. Clark currently lives in the North Texas Hill Country with her precious pups, Beau and Bandit.

For my children: Mike, Gina and Steve,
who are my everything.

Land Above

Chapter One

Benjamin reached the head of the winding staircase overlooking the great hall below; he hesitated a moment to view the gallery of ancestors lining the wall of the stairwell. He remembered how, as a young boy, all the stern, glaring eyes seemed to follow him down the stairs, making him feel guilty for something, something he had probably done. Now, descending, he passed each one and smiled, no longer intimidated by their disapproving gaze. When he reached the foot of the stairs, his boots made a clicking sound against the marble floor, and he knew this would signal his arrival to his waiting parents. Continuing down the hall he passed under a massive 30 foot chandelier casting patterns of light over the frescoed walls and onto the crystal vase of orchids sitting on a table of golden inlay. And then just beyond the parlor, where his parents waited, enormous hand carved doors rose a full twenty feet to the ornate ceiling. The doors came from the old castle, now in ruins, where earlier generations of high born O'Connor's, his mother's ancestors, had lived.

Arriving from Belfast after midnight the night before, Benjamin immediately retired to his room, sleeping restlessly, his body aching from three months at sea and the ten mile carriage ride. Now hearing the voices of his parents in the adjoining parlor, thoughts whirled like waters caught in an ebb tide, thinking and rethinking the words he knew would set off a storm, a storm far fiercer than the many he faced at sea.

Entering the red linen lined parlor, Benjamin kissed his mother and shook the hand of his father. His heart swelled with the admiration and affection he felt for them; Lady Katherine, elegant as always in blue satin and lace, her golden red hair touched with silver, and Sir Edward, with a leather face lined with the many years he served as Admiral in the British navy, now broken in smile for his only son.

"Benjamin, my darling, it is always so wonderful to see you after your time away." Sir Edward helped her to her feet and she held Benjamin's face in her hands, looking at him with adoration, and kissed his cheek. In locked arm they entered the breakfast room; glistening gold silk wall coverings and a long sixteenth century table dressed in white from the linens to the large crystal vase of white lilies from the gardens.

"So, son, did your mission to North Africa prove successful?"

"Yes, Father, we accomplished all the Admiralty expected and more. Hopefully, we'll be able to avoid more conflicts in that region for some time; God knows we've enough trouble elsewhere and at home to keep the navy on alert."

"I believe my replacement at Admiralty is a good man; I envy his job at times and miss being the one formulating these peace agreements."

"You are missed, Father, and everywhere I go the name McLain allows doors to open for me; and you know I moved up faster in ranks due to being your son."

"Nonsense, you are a McLain in your own right; a better head for naval strategy or seamanship would be hard to find."

"Thanks again to you, Father."

Looking at the two men in conversation, Lady Katherine, pretending great affront said, "I wish to change the conversation now my dears, you know I never pretended to like the fact that after so many years married to a naval man, I would also have a son so employed. Edward you know Benjamin would have become a first class statesman after graduating law from Trinity, but, no, like father like son and off he goes to sea."

Benjamin finished a breakfast scone and another cup of coffee, pondering his mother's remarks and knowing it had become time to speak his mind.

"I've put off telling you my plans for too long." He hesitated only a moment, "This afternoon I'm asking Anna to marry me. Our friendship has developed deeper roots over the past couple years. I love her and hope you will grow to love her too."

"No, no, it cannot happen," said Lady Katherine. "I knew something awful would come from your friendship with those Campbell's. Good God, Benjamin, they are Protestant planters leasing land from the British. Oh, you cannot be serious about this."

"Mother, you are aware Theodore Campbell left Scotland because the British ruined the economy of Scotland with high taxes. He left so he could continue to provide for his family; the relocation of Scottish farmer's to Northern Ireland provided a measure of security.

"Of course I know that and I know our lands were confiscated by England and given to these planters."

"Yes, and your estate is one of the few left owned by anyone of true Irish ancestry."

"As I said, these low blooded immigrants took over Irish lands."

"First of all, Theodore owned a plantation in Scotland; perhaps not a castle built by barons and earls, as is your O'Connor estate, but one of prestige in the area of Dumphries. He, his wife, Mary, Liam and Anna lived well and the Campbell bloodlines include Robert the Bruce. You have nothing to look down on; the Campbell's are an honorable family."

"So you say."

"No, Mother, so be it. And don't blame the immigrants; blame the English who devised a way to rule Northern Ireland."

"But, the Campbell's are still not Irish nobility, and you are of that bloodline. You are breaking my heart; all my hopes and dreams for you are dying away; first going to sea and then this." Lady Katherine leaned back in her chair, her long curls falling across her brow. No matter how she suffered she would not lose her dignity.

Breaking the silence Sir Edward said, "Benjamin, surely you know by now your mother's wish for you a marriage to continue her line of nobility, she will persist in this adventure until it is accomplish; be patient my son." He lifted his coffee to his lips"

"You two need not think I am only concerned about continuing the O'Connor line through my one and only child; I tend to other serious matters, like enabling your course habit of drinking coffee. She mockingly lifted her cup of English breakfast tea.

"Another reason, my dear, you resent the navy; course coffee drinkers." Sir Edward said with a raise of his cup back to her."

"Mother, I'm sorry I can't please you, but it's important for me to have you meet Anna. When may I bring my betrothed for dinner?"

"Don't speak of being betrothed Benjamin. There are customs to follow, we must meet and approve of your choice and I am determined this will not be your choice. Edward, tell him not to be so unkind to his Mother." Lady Katherine began sipping her tea looking away from both of them.

Edward sat quietly, nodding slightly towards Benjamin and continued eating his breakfast.

"Mother, you can't in good faith say you'll not accept my love for Anna; you've always been there for me when it mattered and this matters more than anything in my life, as I love her and want her to be my wife, please be reasonable."

"Benjamin, I did not say I would not accept your feelings for Anna, but as your mother you must realize I know what is best for you and will bring you happiness in the future; alas, dear boy, I must warn you of the danger I foresee if you continue to follow the course you have set upon."

"Mother you irritate me no end, why do you think you have all the answers for my life; can you not see your feelings are related to your own perilous grip on a lifestyle that is slipping away?"

Lady Katherine, sitting straight and regal, looked young for her fifty-five years, with lovely fair Irish skin and royal blue eyes, now sparkling with a sharp glint at her son. Benjamin knew why his father had loved her all these years; such loveliness turned a man's head, and aside from her obsession about her royal blood, her overall demeanor exhibited a warm and generous spirit.

They sat silently through the meal and upon arising Lady Katherine, with a look of resignation, said, "Next Saturday will be good time for me. Bring your Anna for dinner and perhaps afterwards she will grace us with some piano music, if she is as good as you say."

"I will ask her, and thank you. I'm sure you will grow to love her as I do." And then closing his eyes a minute knowing how much pain his next sentence would bring to his father, he said, "I've turned in my naval commission and will leave after my next voyage. Last spring I made an offer on the Edward's Estate, adjoining you to the south, and the paperwork will be signed soon."

Sir Edward sat stone still; the stern features hardened and his jaw clenched. Benjamin knew the great disappointment he must feel, always assuming his son would climb the ranks to the Admiralty as he had. The silence seemed unbearable and then he spoke. "Benjamin, you must live your life your way not my way or your mother's way. I will always support your decisions and your mother will too."

Returning to his room after breakfast, Benjamin's thoughts skipped to earlier times. He remembered vividly his mother's words; "Benjamin is determined to make my life miserable," he would hear over and over, as Lady Katherine pretended anguish over her adored son; but he knew in fact this was her way of saying she thought him a determined young man who could wrap her around his finger without effort by knowing when to show the affection and loyalty she demanded and at the same time removing himself from her tendency to entangle him in her airs of pretention.

How many times had he been sat down in that big chair in the library, beginning when his young boy feet didn't reach the floor, and often during his early school days, when he squirmed and fidgeted until she demanded he look at her, and repeating so many times; "Benjamin you must meet more girls of yours own class; Benjamin, I will not allow you to keep visiting that neighbor boy, Liam. He is a planter's son and not proper company for someone of your bloodline; Benjamin, you can not go to sea as your father, you must be landed gentry, as your O'Connor ancestors." So many times over the years he heard these demands, he learned to shut them out.

Changing to his riding clothes, he bade his parent's farewell, explaining his visit to Anna. In the stables he found Lightening, his faithful white stallion, readied for the mile and a half trip to the Campbell's. "Cal, you always anticipate my needs and I thank you," he said to the stable hand that had been with the estate for most of his life.

"Sir, Lightening has been pacing and prodding every since you arrived last night He always senses your presence. I've kept him exercised and healthy, but it is you he longs for."

"Yes, we have a close bond; he means everything to me and I'm so glad to be riding him again and off that damned rolling ship. Thanks for keeping him fit for my return."

On Lightening, man and beast soon found their rhythm, and as the cloudy morning relinquished its hold, the sun played its ritual with shadow and light across the landscape and began to bring the spring colors into play. Benjamin loved his home land; from early boyhood he had ridden and played in this environment; close to the rugged sea shore, where the air always had a nose of salt; fresh and at times stringent, and the land arising from the rocky shore benefited from the rains produced by the clouds full of moisture.

Benjamin's thoughts once again rested with his mother. He realized she loved her husband, Sir Edward, with a devotion unexplained by their differences; her only requirement before their marriage related to his promise to raise their children as young lords and ladies in the Catholic faith. Benjamin, as it turned out, enjoyed the privilege, in his mind, to be their only child and he knew from the time he could walk he wanted to go to sea like his father. His mother always said, with his strong but loving nature and handsome good looks, he would find life came easy to him and she would be powerless to object to his demands; what Benjamin wanted, Benjamin got and he wanted to go to sea and now, a smile crossing his thoughtful face, he wanted to spend the remaining days of his life with Anna.

The thought of Anna brought the remembrance of how he met her once again at his friend Liam Campbell's home one late afternoon soon after graduation from University. As Benjamin entered the gate leading to the small, white, vine covered bungalow, a beautiful young lady approached on horseback from the opposite direction. Her windblown, long dark hair and remarkable hazel eyes greeted him; "Remember me, I'm Anna."

Benjamin stood dumb struck. Could this petite, lovely creature be Liam's younger sister who had been away at school in Scotland? "It can't be Anna, the little girl with big teeth?" He smiled and could not stop staring at her.

And now once again, four years later, he approached the Campbell front gate and rushing towards him, her dark hair falling loosely on her shoulders, saying, "Benjamin, oh Benjamin," and quickly he alighted from Lightening and her long awaited warmth filled his arms.

During that summer of 1769, his twenty-fifth year, Anna and Benjamin spent as much time as possible together. They often rode their horses across the rolling green Irish landscape and upon reaching the coast, tied up their steeds, descended a path leading to a rocky cove where they would sit holding hands and watch the sea push over and around big boulders before reaching shore.

Now, as he held Anna anew, he whispered, "Let's go riding my dear. I want to visit our special cove with you once again." She led him through the rough hewn front door leading into the white vine covered cottage.

"You visit with father while I change into my riding clothes," she reached up to kiss him quickly and he saw Theodore sitting in the far corner in his big chair by the fireplace. When he recognized Benjamin he rose and extended his hand, "My boy, how good to see you again. It seems too long since your last visit."

"Yes, sir, it seemed too long to me too. I just told my father about how I planned on relinquishing my commission after my next voyage. He took it well, although I know he felt great disappointment. I'm in the process of purchasing the Edward's estate and, Sir; I want to ask your daughter to marry me."

Theodore smiled and said, "I expected you to ask for Anna's hand, but I'm very pleased you will not be away at sea so much for the sake of Anna and future grandchildren. Since you and Liam played together and later helped me in the fields, I knew your heart could be of the land. Good for you son, and I give you my blessing to ask Anna to marry you."

"I'm ready, let's go," said Anna, as she reappeared looking lovely in her riding breaches and tall boots; Benjamin once again taken aback by her natural beauty.

The horses, feeling a free rein, galloped along the trail burning off energy. Approaching the shore, where the morning fog had burned off and the sea sparkled amazingly blue with silvery caps breaking against the craggy shore, they tied the horses, and carefully found their way down the steep, rocky path to the small, sandy cove they now called their own. Side by side, holding hands once again, they listened to the cry of sea birds and the surf pounding against the high cliffs surrounding the cove. Benjamin, feeling somehow caught up in the wonder of the moment, brought Anna close and said, "Anna, I love you so much and want to spend the rest of my years with you by my side, please marry me?"

Anna sat silent, for too long thought Benjamin, and then spoke, "Dear Benjamin, I love you very much and I know your mother has made a good marriage with your father, even though he spent so long at sea, but if we marry, I long for both of us to raise our children together."

"I'm planning on resigning my commission after my next voyage. I told your father about it before we left your place, I asked for your hand in marriage and told him I'm purchasing the Edward's estate and I want us to be there together. Please say you'll marry me, my love."

Still resting in his arms and looking into his expectant eyes, she said, "I love you and want nothing more than to be your wife, but I fear your mother will not accept you marrying a commoner."

"Anna, dear Anna, please understand I love you and my life is in my hands, not my mother's. She ran away with my Scottish father, Edward McLean, a lieutenant in the Royal Navy, when she was only seventeen, and her mother never forgave her for marrying an outsider, but at his death her father willed the estate to her; beseeching her to hold fast to her heritage. She has held on with a tightening grip ever since."

"Benjamin, my father doesn't take kindly to being looked down on; he is proud of our heritage, and although he likes you and believes we could be happy together, he is afraid your mother will always stand between us."

"My mother is a very determined woman, but she loves me and I believe in time she will understand my happiness is to be with you; please my love; say you'll marry me when I return from my next voyage."

"Let's give it a little more time, my darling." With her tender smile and a warm embrace, Benjamin felt helpless to press her further.

After they arrived back at the Campbell house and put Anna's horse in the hands of the stable boy, Benjamin said, "My parents asked me to invite you and your father for dinner next Saturday. Will you please come?"

"Father is planning a trip to visit Liam and Elizabeth in Belfast. Liam has been gone so much since he joined the merchant fleet, father is anxious to see him. They're expecting their second child soon; but I'll gladly join you."

"I'm so happy you'll come. I'll bring the carriage by at five, if that's okay with you?"

"I look forward to it." On tiptoe she kissed him soundly, then turned, gave him a reassuring smile, and disappeared through the door.

On the way home, Benjamin exclaimed to Lightening, "Old boy, I've never felt so vulnerable before; I've fought our country's enemies, battled storms at sea, and clashed with a determined mother, but have never felt such dread. I can't lose what I want most of all, the rest of my life depends on it."

Chapter Two

The next Saturday, Benjamin drove the carriage for Anna; Theodore, standing large with his ruddy complexion and thatch of gray hair, stood waiting for him at the front gate. "Lad, you take care of my girl, don't let her be hurt by anyone attempting to make her less than she is; she is a fine lady, born from bloodlines reaching to Clan Lamont's and King Robert the Bruce; she is as royal as any of you; don't forget that my son."

"Sir, she will be treated with respect and accepted by my family. I would not take her any place where she was not treated like the lady she is. My mother has requested to hear her play the piano for them, and I know she will love Anna, as I do, when she gets to know her. As you know, my father is a Scotsman, like you, and Anna will warm his Scot heart. Fear not, Sir, she will be safe with me. And, please give Liam and Elizabeth my greetings and best wishes when you see them.

Benjamin entered the well kept cottage warmed by the glow from the fireplace lighting an arrangement of worn but comfortable davenports and chairs and Anna's spinet piano sitting against a white stucco wall, with a portrait of a lovely lady closely resembling Anna hanging above the piano; noticing Benjamin's gaze, Theodore said, "That's Mary, Anna's mother. Liam and Anna were very young when she died."

"I know, Liam and Anna have talked about her so much. I'm sorry for your loss, Sir. You've been a good father."

"I could only do my best."

Anna entered the living room, lovely in a pale cream colored satin dress, fitted high above her waist; her lovely bosoms graced by a mother of pearl pendent, her shining chestnut hair hung loose in back, the sides upswept and held by jeweled combs. As he wrapped her shoulders in a warm shawl, he whispered, "I fall in love again every time I see you."

She smiled knowingly and letting her gaze drift down him, "And you make my heart race in your elegant waistcoat and shinning boots, my love."

"Whatever you have to say you can say in normal voices," scolded her father with a grin. "Young lad, you take care of my girl and keep those horses on a slow pace; they look a handful, shaking their heads and pawing the ground."

"I'll drive safely sir, the team likes to show off, but they are well behaved underway." He helped Anna up on the seat and jumped in next to her. "We'll see you later this evening Mr. Campbell."

Anna's father stood silently as they drove off, hands in his pockets, proud of the beautiful young daughter, who looked so much like her mother.

The road leading to the O'Connor Estate traversed a countryside rich with black soil and early spring crops. Alternating between the fields, pastures of grasses providing victuals for the grazing cattle readying for spring calving and up ahead on the right were pastures and barns for the beautiful white horses Katherine prized; half Egyptian Arabian and half bloodlines from the royal Lipizzaner stallions, a mixture which created a larger horse than pure Arabian with the intelligence, beauty and swiftness of the Arabian. Benjamin loved these horses of Lightning's lineage.

The winding tree lined road crossed several bridges over clear running streams, and then after the mile and a half trip from Anna's place, they pulled in front of the elegant mansion built by O'Connor's to replace the earlier castle. Sir Edward and Lady Katherine waited at the top of the marble steps and as Benjamin and Anna approached, Sir Edward greeted Anna with a warm embrace. "You are as lovely as Benjamin described, welcome to our home." Lady Katherine extended her cool hand to Anna and embraced her son.

"Thank you for having me, Sir Edward and Lady Katherine. Benjamin has told me so much about you." Benjamin escorted Anna to a chair in the parlor and stood by her side; his parents sat side by side on a curved red velvet divan, over which a large portrait of Katherine gazed down on them. The parlor, with its red silk walls, damask upholstery, lovely tapestries and Persian rugs, glowed, as though the ambers from the elegant marble fireplace insisted on highlighting the silk and taffetas of the ladies gowns and the cravats of the gentlemen.

"Dear, you are from Scotland I understand. My family comes from a long line of Scots from the southwest lowlands, Dumphries to be exact. May I inquire of your birth home?"

"We are from the same area, Sir Edward, only further east. The Campbell's have a long tradition in this area, I suppose you know that?"

"Oh yes, the name is very familiar going back to Clan Campbell.

"I've not been too interested in our family genealogy; however, father says the Campbell's were directly related to King Robert the Bruce. I understand the McLain's have large ancestral estates in Scotland."

"Yes, that is true."

Lady Katherine, sitting quietly through this conversation, seemed absorbed in studying the presence of Anna. "Benjamin don't stand there as if protecting the dear girl; please be seated, and Anna, while talk of Scotland seems appropriate, I am much more interested in Benjamin's roots here in Ireland, as my family has deep roots going back to the first kings and queens, and I am deeply troubled by Benjamin's neglect of my side of the family."

"Mother, I don't understand what you mean; although my surname is McLain, you have never let me forget the O'Connor half. Look around, there are O'Connor's looking down on us from every wall, oh yes, Mother, it is difficult to neglect your side of me."

"Don't be clever Benjamin; I am serious. You have always chosen the McLain side, going to sea and now wanting to be a planter and your interest in a planter's daughter. I am sorry Anna, if that sounds cruel, but I have always guided Benjamin towards his noble responsibilities. I don't want our important heritage to come to a halt with Benjamin not fulfilling his obligations."

"You certainly have a right to influence your son's choices, Lady Katherine, but Benjamin tells me he is able to decide for himself his destiny. I love your son, but I would never stand in his way in being what he is meant to be."

"And that is what this is about Mother, I am meant to be with the woman I love and I have chosen Anna. Please know you can't influence me further in this manner."

As the conversation ended with looks of tension all around, the butler, dressed in black and a stiff white collar, entered and announced, "Dinner is served, Lady Katherine."

"Forgive me, if I have been out of line, dear ones; let us enjoy our dinner together." With a warm look, Lady Katherine led the way to the elegantly attired table sitting under a century's old Waterford chandelier with Irish laced table arrayed with fine china, crystal, and silver service, along with lovely flowers from the garden presented in low crystal vases.

"I hope you found dinner to your satisfaction," Lady Katherine said, after dinner, as they entered the large library that extended the length of the west side of the mansion. "I thought we would have some port here. Anna, would you please play for us? Benjamin tells me you play very well and our piano has gone begging for a sonata to warm its keys."

"The dinner was delicious, Lady Katherine, and I'll be pleased to play for you whenever you desire."

"Port is served Madam," said the butler carrying the silver tray with crystal snifters filled with the amber red liquid.

Seated in the large library, surrounded by bookcases and facing a colossal fireplace whose stones came from the original castle built by Irish artisans for a noble king O'Connor, Benjamin, sipping his port, said, "Father, I would like you to go with me tomorrow, if possible, to see the land I finally signed the papers on this week; your opinion in regard to my planting ideas would be greatly appreciated."

"Well Benjamin, at heart I remain more of a sailor than farmer, but I would like to see the land, I understand it is a large enough parcel to offer you a fine living. Do you plan on building on it soon?"

"Yes, I've recently received the plans from the architects and have talked to some builders and I hope to begin as soon as I return from this last voyage." Benjamin looked over to Anna and reached for her hand. "You know I've asked Anna to marry me when I return?"

Lady Katherine said, "Son, you are so impetuous. Anna should be hesitant about marrying into a family with such noble attributes, she would find it difficult to adjust; I am sure."

Mother, you're wrong; Anna is as noble as we, and further this heritage you continually speak of is not important to us. You know with England ruling Ireland, the Irish noble is a thing of the past. Give it up, Mother; for God's sake you make such a deal about nothing."

"Benjamin, we are rude speaking in front of Anna this way." They sat quietly and found comfort in the group of leather divans and chairs fronting the large fireplace aglow with fresh logs. After finishing their port, Lady Katherine said, "Are you ready to play for us, dear?"

"Yes, if you wish." Arising, Benjamin helped Anna to her feet and walked with her to the elegantly carved grand piano. She, carefully placing her gown under her, sat for a minute as if in contemplation. Benjamin knew she felt hurt over his mother's remarks, and he wanted to comfort her; he touched her shoulder gently and sat in a chair closer to the piano.

Anna began with a Pachelbel, deftly moved into a lively Bach and concluded with an Allegro by Mozart; a hush followed until Benjamin went to her side and lifting her hands to his lips kissed them softly, "You play so beautifully," he said, his eyes full of pride.

Sir Edward echoes his words and Lady Katherine said, "Anna, you must have had a good maestro; an Englishman?"

"I studied with a teacher in our home town, a Scotsman. I entered the local academy of arts at fifteen and attended classes there for two years before we came to Ireland, and then I returned to the University of Glasgow to study for four more years.

"My Benjamin graduated from Trinity University in Dublin, receiving a certificate of law. Seems neither of you used your education for advantage."

"Perhaps we will later in life," Anna said glancing to Benjamin.

"Yes, we have a long life ahead of us Mother."

"Am I to understand your father raised you from childhood?" Sir Edward asked.

"Yes, my mother died before my sixth birthday. My brother Liam had just turned eight."

"Your father did well for you my dear."

Benjamin helped Anna from the leather piano bench. "I need to get Anna home now; I promised her father I would not be too late." Benjamin retrieved Anna's shawl; putting it around her shoulders, as she expressed her gratitude for a lovely evening. Benjamin, who had ordered the carriage earlier, helped her into the black buggy. As the horses pranced along the tree lined road in the pale light of the quarter moon, Benjamin attempted to make conversation with Anna, who sat quietly next to him. "I'm sorry if mother seemed rude. Her obsession in regard to her family's royalty is irritating at best."

Anna remained silent until they reached the entry gate leading to the white cottage. Benjamin stopped the horses and with a soft voice, she said, "Benjamin, please hear me and try to understand what I say; I don't want to hurt you, but I don't want to be hurt. Even though I believe we love each other, I once again repeat, time will not be kind to us. Your mother is too strong in your life for her not to cause problems. It breaks my heart to say it, but I will not marry you." She wiped away tears and pulled her shawl tighter around her, as if to stop the shaking.

"But...."

"No, Benjamin. I don't want to discuss it further. Please help me down and let's go on without each other." Reaching the ground she dashed up the front porch steps, looked back with tears flowing down her face, then opened the door and disappeared.

Chapter Three

The cloudbank, black with rotating, tumultuous winds, appeared rapidly on the eastern horizon; the men had but minutes to lower the sails before it caught them in its ferociousness. The sea picked up rapidly and began to swirl and pitch its white foamy waves against the port side and over the decks; the ship listed so far to stern the sailors could only hold tight to whatever they could. Soon the violent storm wrapped them in its strong blow and heavy rain and left them but a ghost ship lost to its fate.

****

A beautiful young lady, her full flowered dress flying about in the sea wind, shouted, "Help, help, I need someone to help me." She continued running towards the small village and soon encountered her brother, Kylan. She spoke in her native Norwegian tongue, "Help me, I found a body in the rocky cove under the big rock. I think he is alive, we need to get him to the house." Her brother returned with her and they climbed down over the big rock to find the body.

"We will need help to move him, Elina "Wait here, I'll get father's wagon; we can pull him down to the sand and then bring him around the rock." He ran back towards the village and returned shortly with a long wooden wagon on wheels.

"Be careful with him, he may have fractures, he hasn't been on the beach very long; I walked here yesterday morning looking for shells."

With much effort the young lady and her brother loaded the unconscious man on the wagon; his ragged clothes revealed bare arms and legs covered with scraps and bruises. "Thank God you are so strong Kylan." They finished lifting the body into the cottage, and into a cot located in a small back room. She took off the wet remnants of clothing, drying his cold, bruised body with a towel and wrapping him tight in a large blanket, like a swaddled child. "I don't see any fractures; let's keep him warm and try to get something down his throat. Maybe he will wake soon, and then we can decide if he needs a doctor."

Elina sat next to the cot and couldn't stop gazing at the handsome face of the unconscious man; his muscled body, a head of thick dark hair, and sparser body hair, she thought him in his mid twenties. She had often seen her brother's body as they grew up together, but somehow seeing this stranger's naked body brought physical feelings she had not yet experienced in her seventeen years.

On the second day Benjamin stirred; emitting a low sound he suddenly sat up in the small bed. Elina came running into the room and heard him say something in English, but upon seeing her he fell back on the cot and closed his eyes. Elina had studied English in school, and she said, "It's alright, you are alright, just washed up on the beach and we brought you home. Do you hear me?"

Benjamin heard the voice and attempted to focus. Washed up on a beach, it didn't make sense, why would he be on a beach? He couldn't remember anything, even his name or what happened to land him on a beach. He felt pain, opened his eyes and looked down at his body wrapped tight in bed clothes; struggling to get lose, he heard, "I'll help you, I wanted to keep you warm." She rolled him easily one way and then the other and his arms became free. "I made some chicken soup; let me help you get some down, it will make you stronger."

She put a stack of pillows under his head and sat next to him, spoon feeding the soup into his hungry mouth. All he could do is look at her with inquiring eyes as he ate with great hunger. "You are getting color back. I worried you needed a doctor, but we only have an old man who visits the village every other week. What name do you have?"

Benjamin looked at this very pretty young lady with the large blue eyes full of questions. As if suddenly remembering, he said, "My name is Benjamin, what is yours?"

I'm Elina. My brother Kylan helped me bring you to the house after I found you on the beach. You must have washed up overnight. Were you in a ship wreck?"

It came back in small segments; first the storm and trying to keep the ship steady, then knowing it couldn't be saved, and soon being in the water, finding a large piece of floating debris to hang onto and crying out for his mates; and there the visions stopped. Oh God, he thought, did others make it to safety? He slept, ate and Elina brought him a wash bowl each day with hot water and a covered commode, which he saw Kylan take and empty each morning. As he got stronger, Elina helped him out on the porch to sit in the sunshine.

"Elina, do you and Kylan live alone?"

"No, my father is out to sea, he will be back when the tank is full; he is a fisherman."

"Where is your mother?"

"She died shortly after Kylan was born and I three."

"So you have been mother to Kylan and caretaker for your father?"

"I guess so, but don't think of it that way. My father has taken good care of us. Do you want to talk about you?"

Benjamin told her about the shipwreck and that North Ireland was his home. He didn't talk about his family or life there; he realized his past felt dead to him.

Benjamin soon learned the small Norwegian island, where he washed ashore, sat about five miles off from the mainland; the coastal side rugged with gray, rocky shoreline washed by the North Atlantic Ocean and warmed by the Gulf Stream running close to shore, further west green topped hillsides connected to fertile pastures. The Islanders fished from the abundance of sea life in the surrounding waters, and farmers provided dairy, vegetables and fruits to fill the local market. Elina and Kylan's small whitewashed cottage, weathered from the constant sea breeze, sat on the far edge of a small village where the fishing fleet docked.

After Benjamin found strength for a daily walk, Elina took him on paths leading north along the shoreline. She showed him her favorite small inlet where dolphin's played and whales blew their spouts far out in the calm waters; here he found solitude, with a breath of serenity, he had often longed for. Now that he remembered his past, he thought about the cove he and Anna had visited; putting it out of his mind as rapidly as it appeared.

Benjamin often found more pleasure in watching Elina's exuberance than the sights she brought him to see. He had never been with anyone so free and spirited; her laughter would ring out over the smallest bird song, or her smiling eyes would find him and with her finger to her mouth, keep him quiet until he could see a bird building her nest in a rocky cave. Benjamin had often heard Norway called the 'Masterpiece of Nature' and now he knew why. This small peaceful island, with all its channels and harbors, offered endless landscapes to captivate the senses, and if Elina was an example, spirited people free from artificial formality, self-importance or arrogance.

"Elina," Benjamin said, as they sat on a large rock overlooking her favorite inlet, "How old are you?"

"I'm seventeen, but will be eighteen soon."

"When did you learn to speak English so well?"

"During my school days my father sent me to live with my mother's sister in Oslo. Kylan has been going there too, and will return in the fall."

"Do many of the villagers speak English?"

"No, very limited. Some have learned from visiting seaman, but they don't practice it much. My father speaks a little English and is learning more all the time. How old are you Benjamin?"

"I turned twenty-five a few months back; do I seem awfully old to you?"

Elina smiled with her sparkling eyes gazing intently on him;" No, you look young, my father is old."

"You are a diplomat at heart," and he laughed. They remained quiet and Benjamin felt more peace than he had for some time.

In the distance, over the sea sound, they heard someone shouting in Norwegian, "Elina, come home, father is back."

She stood waving her arms for him to see. "You will like my father, he knows no stranger."

"I'll be glad to meet him." They started back down the path leading to the village and as they approached the whitewashed house, a large man in fisherman coveralls stood leaning against the door removing his long rubber boots and Elina broke out into a run; they embraced warmly and noticing Benjamin following along back of her, said, "Kylan told me of you, you look well young fellow."

"Yes Sir, thanks to your son and daughter; they saved my life. You can see I am wearing your clothes and have been eating your food, I hope you will let me make it up to you."

"Call me Ivar. I understand you man of sea?"

"Yes, I spent four years on an English naval ship. I resigned my post to take effect after this last voyage; the ship must be missed by now and I wonder if any of the crew has been found. I need to go to Oslo soon and make contact.

"News travels slow on island, or mainland. In three months Kylan and Elina return to school in Oslo; we will take boat then; can you wait that long?

"I will attempt to get a message off to the naval station in Oslo and wait until you can find me transport or go with you in three months. Until then maybe I can work off my room and board by working on your fishing boat?"

"Maybe you go with us next trip; we always need strong hand on deck."

"Thank you, Ivar, it would be my pleasure, I've been feeling landlocked and am ready for sea legs again. How soon do you go out again?"

"This time of year when sea calm we stay in only to unload and rest day or two. I hate leaving Kylan and Elina alone so much, but need money and keep busy schedule before strong winds of winter."

They had entered the mudroom, hung up their coats, and in the main room they found comfortable, well made Scandinavian wood furniture with cushions covered in sheep's wool, a large wool rug stretched in front of the native rock fireplace, stacked full of logs set aglow by Kylan. "You do fine fire, son." Ivor patted his fourteen year old's leg saying, "Son, you grow like weed, you tall like me. Maybe you and Elina go fishing next time; has been long time."

"Oh Father, we would love to go out, wouldn't we Kylan?

Kylan nodded and gave a big lopsided smile.

Ivar said, "We do it, be ready day after tomorrow."

Elina went to the kitchen which overlooked the large living room. Kylan had placed an iron cook pot of mutton stew, she had made earlier, on the arm of the rod in the fire pit, and she quickly rolled out some biscuits and placed them in the wood stove oven. "Father, are you ready for your evening grogg? I can make a couple of mugs for you and Benjamin."

"Yes, my cold hands like hot mug, and my belly like hot drink." Ivar smiled the same open smile with sparkling eyes Benjamin loved in Elina, and a warmth came over him; a warmth of comfort with this Norwegian fishing family. They sat quietly studying the fire, a silence that spoke of home.

Two days later the early morning fog lifted off the water as their boat headed due west at first light with Benjamin at the wheel, while Ivar, and his experienced crew of Kylan and Elina, raised the sails and began readying the fishing net and equipment. Stopping work for a minute, Ivar turns to his daughter, "Elina, you go galley now and fix coffee and fish cakes – must keep energy up."

After energizing with plates of fish and vegetable pastries, served with strong black coffee, Benjamin headed the 35 foot fishing sloop into the wind to halt its progress under sail, while Ivar and crew lowered the fishing nets into the calm water. Memories of the fatal ship wreck and a very different day at the wheel fleeted through his mind, but the activity on deck quickly changed the scene; he had gone to sea with his father since he was a young boy, but had not experienced work on a fishing boat. They had the fishing nets in the water and would now drag the long net until late afternoon. Benjamin offered to take the first watch; he felt excited about everything and knew he would not be able to nap. Ivar went below to study his charts and rest and Kylan followed him.

"You look pleased with yourself." Elina said as she entered the wheelhouse and sat on a stool. "I noticed you watched everything we did out on deck, maybe tomorrow I can stay at the wheel and you can help father and Kylan."

Benjamin looked at the young lady, dressed like a fisherman, with clothes hanging loosely on her small frame; long rubber boots and a wool cap pulled down over her ears; long blonde curls peeping out and hanging down to her shoulders. "You look pleased with yourself, too," he said smiling. "I'd really like to be a deck hand tomorrow; I'll ask your father about it tonight."

The routine of each day seem to thread nicely into the next and then the next and Benjamin became one with the ship. On their second week out, Elina sat with him in the wheelhouse; the seascape surrounded them with silvery blue water, sea birds of many varieties, all capped by a high blue sky, as the boat, on short sail, pulled the long nets through the water. Elina, watching him as he propelled the boat, noticed how he had grown a dark beard and longer hair, showing under his woolen cap; and yet, even with a somewhat unkempt look and baggy fishing coveralls, the tall, lanky body, she had viewed in its nakedness, aroused desires she wanted to conceal from him. Breaking the silence, Elina said, "The weather in southern Norway is quite balmy, compared to our northern regions, but the sea breeze is cold today, I'm glad you have been able to wear father's clothes; jackets, woolens and all.

"I like the comfort of this clothing; the wool is soft and comfortable. I suppose they dress differently in Oslo?"

"Yes, I think our upper classes dress like the English or Irish ladies in long dresses, men in tight fitting pants with high boots and long waistcoats. I think the men wear more ruffles on their shirts than women do on their dresses." She smiled and added quickly, "Do you have a lady waiting for your return?"

Benjamin remained silent. Elina's abruptness always caught him off guard. He thought of the last night with Anna. He remembered how awful his mother had acted towards her; she was hurt; but did she mean what she said? He remembered how on that last voyage from Belfast, he had thought about that night over and over. He finally said, "I loved someone very much, but it's over now. I don't even have the heart to return to Ireland at the moment. Maybe I'll change my mind when we go to Oslo, lord time is flying by; can't believe June is about over, was it mid-May when you found me and how long before your father returned?"

"You were in bed for a week, and recuperating for two weeks, before father's return. I wish you wouldn't plan on leaving us; there is much you could do here with us. Father likes you and when the salmon run he makes enough money for himself and a crew, but if you didn't want to do that, maybe you could start a business of some kind."

"What kind of business is needed on your small island?"

"Well, I guess I'm not sure about that. Did you ever do anything besides the navy?"

"I helped on our land, and I did plan on being a planter after I left my naval post; but your little island would not do for planting crops, would it?" He smiled and checked his headings, and glanced around in all directions."

"Well actually, we do have some rich soil on the east side of the island. The man that owned the dairy farm moved to Oslo last winter. The village is mostly fisherman, and no one wanted to buy his farm. I think it is still available. He had a small herd to serve the village with milk and cheese and also a large garden. Our summers are short, but the long light days produce abundant crops of carrots, onions and cabbage, which we keep in our cellars over winter and the berries are the sweetest in the world, we always say."

"You are a bundle of facts, and your salesmanship is superb. If I decide to stay longer I promise I will look into land for sale. Did he also have a house there?"

"Oh, yes, a nice whitewashed house like most on the island, but his is a two story with a pretty red tile roof, and being inland is not grayed from the sea winds. His barn and outbuildings are red and his fences are white. He must have made good money to have such a nice place."

Ivar came on deck, "You talk much daughter. I take over now, young man, go below, take food and drink and get rest." Looking at Elina, he said, "You and Kylan check fish tank for ice, we pull nets at five."

Benjamin had some cheese and flatbread and rested in his forward bunk. Ivar called to him at five and the crew began to haul the long, heavy net with the iron wench; after what seemed an eternity, the net toppled the fish onto the large metal tray on the stern; fish jumped and tossed their bodies in the air, sucking for breath and looking for water. "Look, salmon and trout, enough to about fill tank," After throwing back what they didn't want, the metal tray tripped upward and slid the remaining fish into the large tank of ice.

After securing the sails, cleaning the boat, Ivar brought out a bottle of golden akvavit with caraway seed and he and Benjamin sat in deck chairs in the late red and yellow sky of sunset while Elina and Kylan went below to prepare dinner. "Son, what you think of fishing?"

"I've loved ever minute of it. I'm astonished how efficient you are with only three hands; this is a great boat; fishing must pay well."

"Yes, fish here plenty and market good. We Norwegians love our fish."

"Father, dinner is ready." Elina's voice called from the opening to the hatch.

The cabin glowed with a soft golden hue from the light of the captain's lantern, swinging with the motion of the boat, and the aroma of the food cooking in the galley, stirred digestive juices. Elina brought trays of fish balls, boiled cabbage, potatoes and carrots from the galley and sat them family style on the table. Soon the only sound being hungry people eating. When they finished the main course, Elina served a tray of Jarlesberg and liganberry cakes, and more black coffee and akvavit for Benjamin and Ivar.

After helping Elina clean the galley, Benjamin said, "I will sleep like a baby tonight," stretching his arms high above his head.

Ivar said, "I tired too, so will see you in the morning."

After Kylan left for his bunk, Elina looked at Benjamin asking, "Would you like another drink and watch the stars for a little while?"

"Yes, I ate so much. Thank you for such a good dinner; now I need to digest a little before I go to bed."

They climbed the ladder to the hatch, crossed the deck and walked forward to sit leaning back against the rise of the cabin. Benjamin thought he had never seen so many stars; they twinkled brightly like rare diamonds, saying look at me, look at me, I'm the prettiest of all. Suddenly Elina's head lowered to his shoulder. He sat quietly, feeling the soft pressure of her against him; was that his heart he felt pounding? Her breath became regular and he knew she had fallen asleep, he didn't move for fear of waking her; he wanted to soak up the warmth spreading through his tired body for a moment longer.

The fish tank filled in two more days; full of salmon and ocean trout and other varieties. "Usually it would take longer," Ivar told Benjamin, "You good luck, son."

They arrived in port, unloaded their catch; Ivar introduced Benjamin to other fishermen on the dock, and in the distance a voice, so familiar, startled Benjamin. "Hey you, not a ghost I presume." And there on the dock, to Benjamin's dismay, stood Liam.

"Speak of a ghost…." And Benjamin jumped from the deck of the boat to the pier and rushed over to his friend. With gusto they did a manly hug and silently observed one another. "How in the world did you find me on this small, isolated island?"

"I've been helping the navy and your family hunt for you. When my ship anchored in the Oslo harbor, the naval station there confided they had received word you had been rescued on a coastal island. I can't understand why they didn't immediately notify the navy and your family. They said it was a mix up of some sort."

"What about the Captain and the rest of my crew – have any been located?"

"It seems eleven men were saved; but no word has been received about the Captain."

Elina approached the two men and Benjamin introduced her and briefly explained his rescue. "Elina, her brother Kylan and Ivar her father, have given me shelter and work since they found me."

"Your mother and Anna have been desperate to find news of you. They've even formed an alliance; strange how loss brings people together. Will you return with me? My ship sails out of Oslo in five days."

"Now that my rescue has been officially reported, I assume my resignation has taken effect. To tell the truth, I've been so busy here, free from the discord before my last voyage, I couldn't decide if I even wanted anyone to know where I was. But, of course, time heals and I'm anxious to see Anna and family again, but I plan on going to the naval station in Oslo the first week in September, when Elina and Kylan go back to school." Noticing the questioning look on Liam's face, he added, "Did you find my family well?"

"Anna has been miserable, blaming herself for being unkind and not understanding your position in regard to your mother. Things will certainly be better now both of them realize your being alive is more important than anything else." Hesitating for a moment, hoping to hear that Benjamin would change is mind and come with him, "Well my dear friend, I'll be heading back to Oslo tonight, so when I get back home, I'll let Anna and your parents know of your well being and when they can expect to see you again."

"Thanks Liam and give my love to your lovely Elizabeth and Theodore. I'm anxious to see everyone again." They embraced again and parted company.

Elina had moved away to give them privacy, but continued to listen carefully to the conversation. Her heart ached at what she heard, how could he leave them; she loved him, didn't he know?

After dinner, with the golden Akvavit liquor in hand, Benjamin told his companions, of whom he had grown so fond, of his plans to return to Ireland. "I'll miss you; you've been like a family to me. I wouldn't be alive without Elina finding me and helping me to get well."

The family sat quietly for a time and then Ivar said, "Son, we'll miss you too, but understand family in Ireland loves you and wants your return." Elina and Kylan remained silent, staring into the fire.

During the next month Benjamin went to sea often with Ivar and his regular crew; Elina and Kylan remained on shore. When in port, he tried to spend time alone with Elina, to see if he could soften her cool approach towards him; but she remained aloof.

Once while working on the boat in port, he passed by Elina on deck, and said, "Hey, where is that pretty smile?"

Turning to look at him with wide blue eyes, she remained silent and returned to sanding the teak on the deck rails.

"I can't leave believing you are mad at me. You know I'll miss you and hope to see you again someday."

Elina put down the sandpaper and got to her feet, brushing the dust from her baggy pants, she said, "Oh that's just perfect. How long is someday?"

"It isn't easy for us to travel the far distance, but somehow I know there will come a time when we meet again."

"I don't want to meet you again someday. Don't you know how I feel about you? She continued not waiting for a reply, "You always treat me like your young sister. I'm not that much younger than you and I don't feel about you like I do my brother."

"Oh Elina, if only I'd met you first, before my love for Anna, you mustn't pine for me dear one. I'll be devastated if I've hurt you in any way. I've felt our connection too." He studied her sad face, "But it's a different kind of love I feel. You've brought me peace and contentment and a real freedom of spirit with your presence. I'll think of you always."

She looked at him for a minute, then the tears streamed down her face; she ran to the ramp, off the boat, and disappeared in the crowd of the fish market.

Elina did not go with them on the boat to Oslo, deciding to return to university in the spring. She hugged Kylan and said she would see him for the holidays. She gave Benjamin her hand and wished him well and returned to the cottage. Ivar patted him on the shoulder, seeing his distress from Elina's coldness, and they left for the port. It took two days on sail to reach the port of Oslo and on their arrival Benjamin felt sadness when he stepped off the familiar fishing sloop for the last time. He helped Ivar load Kylan's bags onto a waiting buggy and then told them goodbye and watched them drive away. He had never felt such an empty place in his heart before. He had not told Elina the truth about his feelings for her. It was more than brotherly love; but, he felt his obligation to Anna, now especially since he knew she still loved him and would be waiting for his return.

After a restless night's sleep at a boarding house located near the port, Benjamin arose, bathed, shaved and groomed his unruly hair and headed for the naval station to report in. His resignation had been accepted, but they still furnished him with the familiar naval dress; he located his ship and alone in his cabin he glanced in the mirror seeing the Benjamin of old, and yet he knew he would not be that man again. Elina's pretty face passed before his thoughts.

Chapter Four

The weather crossing the Northern Atlantic caused the ship bound for Belfast to change course and pass through the Channel Islands; arriving in Dublin instead of Belfast. Benjamin found coach transportation to Londonderry and on to the estate. It was late afternoon on a cool fall day, the landscape alive with reds, oranges and many shades of gold, when Benjamin came in sight of the crumbling old castle on the cliff, and sitting nearby the grand manor rebuilt and added on to by O'Connor aristocrats over the years, and then his heart skipped a beat as he experienced a feeling of belonging; he had called this home for his first twenty-five years; a toddler picking flowers and being bitten by a bee, a young lad climbing a tall popular tree, falling and breaking his arm; Benjamin smiled to himself; his memories pleasurable in most part.

He saw Joseph, the servant he had known all his life, approach the front steps and soon his mother and father appeared beside him. Benjamin stepped out of the carriage and his mother ran down the steps to his arms. "Benjamin, oh my dear one, oh God, I worried so for you." She stepped back and looked him over, only to rush into his arms again. His father, approached, a smile of joy on his tanned and lined face; reaching around Lady Katherine, he braced his son.

In the parlor, Joseph presented a tray filled for tea time, and the hum of conversation continued through all the questions and answers that followed. "I'm tired now; will you excuse me for a while? I'll rest for an hour or so and then ride over to see Anna. I understand she has attained your favor?"

"Yes, son, we adore Anna; she has been so concerned and afraid for you and she has been very kind to us in our grief. I am sorry I acted as I did. I have been living in the past; I promise things will be different. We love you so, Benjamin, and thank God for your safe return."

Later, fresh and dressed in a riding outfit of tan pants, black boots and brown wool waistcoat, Benjamin had the stable hand bring Lightening; at first sight the white stallion nickered and extended his beautifully shaped head towards its master. Benjamin wrapped his arms around the long neck and patted the silken hair of his nose. He mounted and headed towards Anna's. The twilight shadows illuminated across the road; with evening sounds of nesting birds chirping softy and predator animals scurrying through the brush, foreshadowing nightfall across the countryside where the creatures of darkness pursue prey always alert to danger.

Lightening suddenly nickered, raised his head and spread his nostrils. Benjamin looked around but did not see anything, and then the pounding of horses hooves came from up ahead. Rounding the bend he saw a rider approach at full speed, and then he saw dark hair flowing in the wind and a small body sitting in the saddle, in full control, the excellent rider he remembered.

"Benjamin," she shouted. "Benjamin, is that you?"

"Yes, Anna, it's me." He stepped off Lightening, dropped the reins and came forward, gently lifting her body from her horse. He held her tight and she clung to him, crying softy.

It seemed they would never let each other go. He felt his deep love for this lovely young woman, "Anna, how could I live without you in my arms. How did you know to come and meet me?"

"I ask your mother to send a boy to tell me as soon as you arrived and, oh my love, I couldn't live without you, you'll never know how I suffered, how I wanted to have another chance for our last night together. Please say you forgive me and we'll never be apart again."

"I forgive you, even though there is nothing to forgive. You reacted to things my mother said. She is the one who must seek your forgiveness and I understand she has and she welcomes our life together."

"Yes, oh yes, our life together," She put her head against his chest and he continued to hold her close.

"We must get you home, dear Anna; I won't have you catching your sickness out here in the night." He helped her on her horse, brought Lightening over and stepped up in the saddle; they road along side by side as they had so often that first year of their love.

****

They married in the summer of 1770. In their second year Anna had a baby boy they named William, and two years later Joseph arrived. Now, almost twenty years had passed; at 46 years of age, Benjamin sat at his desk in the large rock home he and Anna had built, reflecting a calm maturity; his dark hair touched with gray about the temples and the deep squint marks of his eyes unable to conceal the glint of his blue eyes.

He now managed the combined estates of Theodore Campbell, his parent's, and his and Anna's estate. Theodore, still active at 79, continued to plant the fields and Lady Katherine, amazingly lovely at 80, and Sir Edward, still resided in their large mansion. William and Joseph, in their teens, attended an academy in Belfast in the winter months and helped on the estate during summer vacations. Benjamin felt surrounded by family and love.

"Anna," he called from his desk, as she passed by in the hallway, still youthful and even more beautiful in Benjamin's eyes, "I need to be in Dublin for a meeting of the legislature early next week, would you want to bring William and Joseph and make it a family outing?"

"I'm sorry dear; don't you remember me telling you father is expecting a visit from his old friend Samuel, the maestro who taught me at the academy. I really look forward to seeing him after so many years."

"Maybe, one of the servants will go with me and I can take the boys to see the sites of Dublin. They could get excused from the academy for this educational venture. After all, they will benefit by seeing the seat of government."

"Are you sure you'll have time to spend with them?"

"My meeting won't take that long; they granted me a hearing on Wednesday morning. Otherwise, our group; representing the moderate planters, both Irish Catholics and Scot and English Protestants, want to be present in the halls to have Government understand our problems here in the North of Ireland. They need to know the radicals of both sides, doom the peace of the region by their night raids, killings and threats. The boys need to begin to understand what is happening in their homeland. It will be their inheritance and livelihood someday."

"I will ask Sara to get the boys packed and have her accompany you and the boys to Dublin."

The carriage loaded with baggage stood ready the next morning and the boys raced to their rooms several times to retrieve some article they forgot; Sara, a large woman with a pleasant smile, had been with the boys since birth; they liked and respected her and Benjamin knew she could keep them entertained on the long journey. Anna stood silently at Benjamin's side until Sara and the boys rested in the carriage. Benjamin held her, kissed her goodbye and stepped up to ride with the driver. He saw Anna standing there still waving as they rounded the bend heading south.

After three nights at roadside inns, the group arrived in Dublin as the sun began to set, casting its pinkish orange glow on the white marble buildings. The boys had never seen such a big and busy city; cobblestone streets vibrated the underside of the carriage and the team neighed hellos to the passing horses. "Father," William, leaning out the open window yelled, "What is that big building over there?"

"Son, that's the Old Library Building of Trinity University where I went to school and where you and Joseph will attend someday. Pretty soon on your right you'll see a large building with many colonnades; that's the Parliament Building, where I speak to parliament tomorrow."

The Inn dominated a corner of the main square; once a residence of royalty. The boys and Sara liked their large rooms; Sara's bedroom had a door entrance to the boys. Benjamin told them to get some rest and he would come for them at dinner time. He wanted to look over his speech one more time and needed to stretch out and get some rest too.

After dinner, served nicely at the Inn dining room, Benjamin took William and Joseph for a walking tour of the city. The lanterns lining the boulevard, filled with whale oil, illuminated the Georgian architecture of the 1700's and Benjamin pointed out the Dublin Castle, Trinity College, the House of Lords, the Parliamentary Building and all the other classical buildings they passed by. He knew the history and sites of Dublin from his early days at university, and enjoyed passing on his knowledge to his wide-eyed sons. After stopping at a market for sweets, they returned to the Inn. "I have to be up early tomorrow; you sleep in and Sara will take you for breakfast. I should be back in a few hours and we can take the carriage to visit some outlying sites."

He soon stretched out on the comfortable goose feather mattress; closing his eyes he thought of Anna. They had been together sixteen years now and it seemed like yesterday. She lived life with great vivacity and charm; enduring the hardships of childbirth with courage and always being a caring mother and loving wife. Lady Katherine had grown very fond of her and they enjoyed each others company. He reached for the extra pillow and held it; he had not slept alone for a long time.

The next day Benjamin stood before parliament and delivered his address firmly, and yet felt he had maintained a reasonable tone in requesting help in the Northern Ireland before the troubles escalated further. He described how radical Protestants burned homes of Irish Catholic farmers and in one case had killed a woman and her two children; but not to be outdone, radical Catholics also raided Protestant farms and terrorized the innocent. The group of ten North Ireland councilmen, ministers, business owners and planters spent the next two hours visiting the offices of state; all beseeching help for their cause. By noon the group left the Parliament Building, gathered briefly to discuss the events of the morning, and then separated, agreeing on a time to meet again after returning to their respective homes in Northern Ireland.

Benjamin walked down to the corner, crossed the street and walked the two blocks to the Inn. He arrived just as a carriage came rapidly around the corner and pulled to a stop in front, the driver jumped down and opened the door of the carriage and out came Theodore Campbell. Benjamin couldn't believe his eye, what on earth, he thought; fear rising in him.

"Benjamin, oh my son." He seemed to murmur and unsteadily reached out for Benjamin's arm.

"What is it Theodore, what's the matter?"

"Take me in to sit down; I don't think I can stand a minute longer."

He helped the stocky older man up the stairs to his room and sat him in a large leather chair; kneeling next to him, he said, "You must tell me what's wrong, what is it?"

"Benjamin, I tried to make her stay overnight, but she wanted to be home. I had my carriage take her home about eight o'clock and Samuel and I stayed up until about ten. Just as I got into bed, I heard a horse and rider approach yelling something." He stopped and put his head in his hands. Benjamin became terrified to hear more; icy cold fingers of fear pushed upon his chest and he thought he would pass out from his terrifying thoughts.

Theodore finally continued, "They burned your house down Benjamin." And then with sobs he couldn't control, he cried, Anna is gone." He stood; fell against Benjamin, and Benjamin, screaming out in pain and wild disbelief, grasp the old man and they fell onto the bed.

In a few moments, they gained some composure and sat up. Theodore continued with tears flowing heavily from his tired eyes, "They didn't stop there, my son, they, they went on, oh my God, and burned your parent's home. Barely able to speak, Benjamin said, "God, no, no it can't be. Please tell me they didn't hurt my mother and father."

Theodore touched Benjamin's shoulder, looking at him with teary eyes. "Yes, they are gone and your man servant and all the rest." Oh son, I am so sorry to tell you this; I came because I felt only I could share your pain, oh, it is too much to bear." He began to sob uncontrollably again and they held on to each other. It seemed an eternity before Theodore finally dozed off. Benjamin sat down in the chair. He knew he must tell the boys and he did not know how he could. In complete exhaustion and despair he wept openly.

Chapter Five

It was in early spring of the year following Anna's death, when Liam crossed from the small boat to shore and began walking towards the fishing pier. He remembered the small village from when he had found Benjamin after the ship wreck; was it close to 20 years ago, he wondered. He asked around for the fisherman who had a 35 foot fishing sloop; he couldn't remember his name. "Oh, you mean Ivar, he should be home. Go down the shore lane and his is the last house on the left." Thanking him, Liam strode swiftly down the road where he entered the gate and knocked on the door.

"Who there?" Came a voice from inside.

"A friend of Benjamin McLain's, Sir. I met you on the pier nearly twenty years ago."

The door opened to reveal Ivar, an old man of seventy, standing erect and alert, still dressed in his fishing clothing, holding a hot cup of coffee. "Benjamin, our friend from Ireland?"

"Yes, that Benjamin. May I come in and visit awhile?"

Ivar led him to the living room, asked if he would like a coffee, and they sat together looking each other over for a while.

"Benjamin has been sick, Ivar. He had a terrible tragedy over a year ago; his wife, my sister, and his parents were all killed.

He can't seem to get over it; by the day he grows more morose. He will not give up his quest to find the raiders who killed his family and burned his home and his parent's home. He intends them great malice. He is in danger from these revolutionaries, but even the love of his sons, doesn't seem to dissuade him from revenge and possibly losing his own life at the same time."

"I'm sorry for your grief; what can I do?"

"I know you and your family made him happy once when he felt alone and hurt. I thought if perhaps your daughter could visit him, he would consent to coming back for a visit and perhaps the sea, the fishing, his friends and the peace he found before could save his life again."

"Elina lives in Oslo now. She teach school there."

"Is she married?"

"She was, he lost at sea two winters ago."

"Would you mind if I went to see her and visit with her about Benjamin?"

Ivar told Liam how to find Elina in Oslo.

After arriving in Oslo, Liam found himself in a well kept neighborhood close to the central park. He walked the street until he came to the house described by Ivar; a cottage behind a white picket fence covered with pink roses. He stepped up to the porch and knocked on the door.

"Who is it?" he heard from within; he noticed the similarities in her father's response and smiled.

"I'm Liam, the friend of Benjamin you met on the fishing pier so many years ago. Has it been almost twenty years?"

She came to the door; at thirty-seven, she still looked very young, her blue eyes remained bright and clear, the soft yellow curls still appeared touched by starlight, and Liam could not find words.

"Liam," she said, "the brother of his fiancé?"

"Yes, Anna was my sister."

"Was your sister?"

"Yes, she was killed in a fire more than a year ago. That's why I'm here; might I not come in and talk with you?"

She opened the door and showed him into a bright and airy room, all soft and comfortable and feminine. "Please sit and I'll get us lemonade and some pastries."

She listened quietly as Liam told her about Benjamin and their concerns. Her eyes never left his, but he could not read her expression. When he had finished, she remained quiet, sipping more of her drink. Finally she said, "I loved him you know. I felt I would die when he left. I didn't marry until twenty-two, and I tried to love my husband, but he deserved more than I could give. I've been alone for two years; he died in a storm at sea. I've found a life that brings me rewards, if not riches, and have adjusted to not having companionship; and now you come with words that can only bring me more pain." She stood and walked to the front window – turning her back to him.

"I'm sorry Elina. I only thought of Benjamin's pain. I remember how he even considered staying in Norway; he told me once if Anna hadn't been waiting for him, he would have wanted to stay with you. Now, I thought you could save him again. I forgot to think how you might feel about the chance of losing him again."

"I'll finish this year's term in two weeks. Please tell me how and where to find Benjamin and I will come. I am strong and once more I will nurse him well again. Do you really believe I can, Liam?"

She stood in the light of the window; her natural, unassuming beauty stunned Liam to silence.

****

Elina's ship arrived in Belfast six months after Liam had visited her in Oslo. "Elina, over here, here I am." He spoke loudly as he saw her disembark the ship and look around the gathering crowd.

"Oh, it's you Liam, so many on the dock. I'm so glad to see your face looking back at me," she said with her lovely smile. "I must look a fright; the ship hit a rough patch this morning and tossed us about. Many got sick. I remained on the deck, in spite of the water spray, and I luckily didn't have any seasickness, but the wind surely did its damage to my hair and I'm kind of wet."

Liam wrapped his arm around her shoulder, guided her through the crowd, and smiled as she rambled on in nervousness. "You look beautiful in all your disarray," he joked. I made reservations at a nice Inn downtown; let's get you there before you catch your death of cold."

Later, after a change of clothes and a couple hours of rest, Elina met Liam in the Inn's dining room. They ordered and Liam smiled noticing how Elina devoured her food; not unladylike, only an ease without pretentions. "We will remain in Belfast, Benjamin is here, has been since the first of the month. We know he's on the trail of those who killed his family and fear for his safety, but he obsesses about them constantly when he's home and finally he told the boys he loved them, but needed to be away for awhile. They thought it meant a goodbye on his part."

"Do you really feel his life is in danger?"

"Oh, yes, these rebels are intent on killing off the Irish and even though Benjamin is only half Irish, he's known as the last of Irish royalty and is a target. I suspect he has disguised his identity in order to get information. I want to find him and hopefully when I tell him you're in Belfast he'll come to see you. Then it will be between the two of you what happens next. Are you sorry I got you into this?"

"No, Liam, it's going to be alright. I know Benjamin will find the answer to his grief; he has a strong constitution and when it comes to right and wrong he'll choose a course that will not bring hurt or shame to his family. He's lost in his anguish, I won't be able to change that, but perhaps the memory of his life in Norway will help change the direction of his thoughts, for a time anyway."

That night Liam wandered from one working class pub to another. Finally in a dark, smoky room he saw a rough looking character at the bar; something about how he stood, tall and erect, and the width of his shoulders got his attention. As he approached he could see a ragged beard and long hair under his black hat; not even that changed the handsome face Liam knew well. Coming up from behind, just as the figure turned to him, he said quietly so not to gain any attention, "Hey old man, don't I know ya?"

"You do turn up at the strangest places." Benjamin looked him over and then patted his shoulder. "Have a whiskey friend."

The pub sat off the street, facing towards a path leading between buildings and connecting to the large road leading to rows of low stone buildings in the manufacturing area of Belfast. Benjamin had been in this area for a fortnight. Dressed in black street clothes, clumpy boots, and a black felt hat pulled down over his eyes, his unshaven face and straggly, dirty looking hair, he felt unrecognizable, even to himself. When he approached the bar to get another whiskey, he spoke with a strong Scottish Gaelic accent to the bartender, using as few words as necessary. He leaned against the wood plank bar, put a foot up on the iron rail, and gave a nod to the bloke sitting on the next stool.

Benjamin had learned a great deal about the revolutionaries he had been attempting to locate since the death of his family. It seemed to him, the only way he would be able to live with the knowledge of his great loss, would be to find the scoundrels and eliminate them in the worst way he could find imaginable. He knew he could do it, every inch of his body and soul would find its revenge; if it killed him, so be it.

He thought of his sons often, feeling guilt; they lost their mother, grandparents, and now a father bent on revenge so deep it would possibly keep him from them too. He had tried to have strength for his sons who had lost so much so young. Theodore insisted they move in with him while they rebuilt their home. It broke Benjamin's heart again every night when he lay in the bed where Anna did as a girl. After a month the boys returned to the academy in Belfast and for a time he rode the country side talking to everyone he could; including those in charge of bringing the raiders to justice. He worked on re-building the large stone house where he and Anna lived, made love, and had children. Eventually, as the pain grew deeper, he began to go to Belfast and make inquiries.

Now with their whiskeys in hand in the dark, smoky pub, smelling sour of drink and sweaty body odors, Liam could only say, "Let's get out of here, I've something to tell you."

On the street, Liam led him down several dark streets until they came to the main road leading into downtown Belfast; there he had parked his carriage and driver to await his return. "Do you have a room someplace where we can get you changed into something decent and maybe shave and trim your hair?"

"Actually my room is only a couple blocks from the next turn. I'd rather not be seen in my regular dress; do you have a room someplace where I can change and clean up?"

"Yes, I'm at the Durham downtown. Bring a bag, you can change there."

After Benjamin retrieved his bag, they proceeded to the Durham where he bathed, shaved and trimmed some hair and dressed. Liam gave him an approving look, "There you are, you look almost human again."

Benjamin seemed pensive and replied, "I know now that being human is not just for the lucky ones with money; there is a whole human race out there that works hard and whose lives are very difficult. It doesn't justify what some of them are doing, but out of ignorance, poverty and hate, they destroy everything that reminds them of their lack."

"You have gained insight by your wanderings, my man." Hesitating, he finally said, "Benjamin, I've news for you. I came looking for you because Elina is here; is right here in a room down the hall. She notified me of her arrival and I came to Belfast to meet her. I told her you are someplace in town, and I would try to find you."

The silence became deafening. Benjamin looked at Liam in disbelief. "I don't understand why she is here; how did she know to come and why did she contact you and not me?"

"We worried about you, Theodore, your sons and I, so early last year when my ship docked in Oslo, I went to the island to talk to Ivar. I thought maybe he could ask you to visit and you would somehow get over your obsession of finding those who killed Anna and your parents, before you endangered your own life."

"You went to the island?"

"Yes, and Ivar suggested I see Elina. He said she lived in Olso and taught school and her husband had died at sea two years before. I told her what had happened to you and that we worried you had no will to live and risked your life to find those responsible for your pain."

"Good God man, why did you want to involve them in this tragedy?"

"Because I remembered how your time in Norway healed your body and mind after the wreck of the ship and your break-up with Anna. I thought maybe your love for Elina and her family could heal you again."

"Where is she?"

"She's waiting to see you. I thought, when you felt ready, I'd take you to her room."

"I'm ready now."

Liam left the room and went down the hall to knock on Elina's door. She answered with a look of expectancy. "Does he want to see me?"

"Yes, but please be patient with him, he seems in shock over everything. It has been a long time since you knew him; I hope you will find him not so much changed."

Elina waited in the silence of her room. She still could not believe she had made this trip to see Benjamin. When he said goodbye, so long ago, she knew in her heart it would never be; the love she yearned for, the touch of his body against hers, a life together sharing their love. Her daydreams had carried her far into this fantasy, a seventeen year old girl's love story; but her heart did not believe it fantasy, she felt love for this beautiful man who had touched her to her depth and somehow she wanted to believe she had touched him too. But he left; "Someday," he had said.

Elina answered the knock at her door. Benjamin stood there before her, his graying temples accenting the lines around his eyes; no longer a young man, but still a very handsome one. Elina stepped forward and with a happy smile reached for his hand. "Dear Benjamin, I'm so delighted to see you again."

He stood holding the warm hand and suddenly reached for her, pulled her close and a sob filled the silence. Elina held tight to him and with soothing sounds said, "I'm so sorry for your loss, so sad for you. I had to see you; I hope you understand my coming to you this way."

He led her to a lounge and sat down next to her. He kept hold of her hand and his eyes seem to devour her. "How beautiful you are Elina, the years have been kind to you. Remember when you found me and I asked if I seemed old to you?" She nodded. "Now you must really think so."

"Silly, you know you are even more handsome." She smiled with her heart, "Benjamin, Liam is worried about you and I think he told you he hoped you might come back to the island for a visit, knowing of your love of it in the short time you stayed with us. I'm hoping I can persuade you to return with me for another visit."

"Dear Elina, I think he also told you of my quest. I can't leave here before I see justice for my family. I've heard a rumor that the English are close to finding these villains. I didn't realize, until a few days ago, English law intended to prosecute them for killing one of their own; my father, a retired Admiral in the British Navy. After they catch them, there will be a trial and hopefully they are brought to justice. Then I've a lot of making up to do to my boys. Do you understand any of what I'm saying?"

"I understand what you have to do; what I don't understand is if you think you will eventually visit us again. If you can, we will welcome you with open arms."

"When they prosecute the killers, and I've some time with my boys, I'd love to visit you, your family and the island again. Until then, won't you come with me to meet my sons and stay a while? My house is not finished, but you would be comfortable in my father-in-laws cottage and he would be very happy to have you."

"Oh, thank you, but no. I only came to see you again and to let you know how you still remain in our hearts. If you'll promise to not take any more risks with your life, I'll book a return back to Oslo as soon as possible. And if the boys would like to come with you to Norway, when you are ready to visit, they'd be welcome."

"You have lifted some sadness and much anger from my heat, dear Elina. Thank you for coming to see me. I promise that if you want it to be, our someday will be soon."

Chapter Six

A year passed from Elina's departure before Benjamin sat in the crowd watching the prosecution case of those who had killed his family; their death by hanging should have brought some relief to his heart, but, he felt somehow it would have been better if he had found them and done his own justice. He wanted to strangle the life out of them with his own bare hands or burn them alive, anything he felt would help cure the burden in his heart, but then he would remember Elina coming all the way to Belfast to wish him well and offer her heart; somehow he needed to go on living, for her and for his sons. He knew he would spend the rest of his years with Elina; seeing her again awoke all the feelings he had kept buried for so long and his love for her would be the only thing to heal the pain residing within. He remembered how for the two days before her ship sailed to Norway they spent each hour, day and night together.

"Benjamin," she had said as he unbuttoned her vest and kissed her neck, "I've longed for this so long; my body has ached for you," His kiss on her lips silenced her and soon they made love like the two young people who had met on that island many years prior. Their great urgency amused them and after the heat subsided they came together again; slower, lovingly caressing and devouring each other.

Afterwards they lie comfortably in each other's arms and Benjamin whispered, "Please say you'll be mine forever, Elina. I love you so very much."

"Yes, Benjamin, I'm yours forever. After the trial and you've spent some time with your sons, please come to Norway. I'll be waiting for you."

That summer when William and Joseph came home for their summer break, they helped Benjamin and hired laborers with rebuilding their house and also to do work on his parent's home; where the main exterior still stood, its gables and spires. Since the fire began in the back, only the interior of the bedrooms where everyone slept burned, thus killing all its occupants; the front rooms and the large library only had smoke damage and many of the portraits and antiques could be restored. It broke his heart to see the lovely portrait of his mother covered with soot, which brought about thoughts of her devastating fate.

The pain he felt at his childhood home became so intense he let others do the work of restoring it. His and Anna's home had burned to the ground. His dear wife and three servants lost their lives; he only rebuilt for the sake of his sons. Now he hoped Elina would feel at home here.

William had always been close to Benjamin; they, so much alike, found comfort in being together, while Joseph, with a nature more attuned to Lady Katherine, often thought his father wrong headed or difficult. Lately Joseph had been spending time with Edith Caulfield, a widow, and her two sons, and wanted his father to get to know the mother. Benjamin had not told his sons about meeting Elina again in Belfast. Long ago he had told them the stories of his time in Norway. He worried his sons might resent his feelings for Elina. Finally, when the time seemed right, he told his sons of his plans for remarrying; William gave him his blessings, but Joseph again told him he should think instead about marrying Edith; their combined estates and wealth paramount in his mind.

Benjamin left in late spring for Oslo, a year and a half from the time he and Elina met in Belfast. They had communicated a few times by post, but he had not heard from her in the last three months. They had made plans to marry on the island and then both return to Ireland. After a stormy crossing, he arrived in Oslo and with directions he received from Liam, he soon located Elina's cottage. It stood empty and he could tell by its appearance no one had been there for some time. His inquiries didn't reveal her whereabouts, so he caught a ship that would bring him to the island. In site of land, Benjamin remembered fondly his days with Elina and her family. He knew the pain of losing Anna could not be diminished, but he had found he could go on living and let her rest in a silent space in his heart; Elina would not be a replacement, but a strong, deeply held love that would grow over the years.

On shore he headed for Ivar's grayed, wind swept house, hoping perhaps he would find Elina there; not the youthful beauty of yesteryear, but a beautiful lady he would ask to marry him.

Ahead he saw Ivar standing on the old porch, "Ivar," Benjamin shouted as he swiftly approached the house. The elderly man turned and faced Benjamin. Twenty years had aged him; Benjamin noticed how his strong shoulders now stooped and his leather lined smiling face drooped.

"It's Benjamin, Ivar. I just arrived from Northern Ireland and I'm looking for Elina. I couldn't locate her in Oslo, her cottage looked vacated."

"Come in, please." Said the old man who turned to go inside; and once inside asked Benjamin to be seated.

The old sofa still had indentions where he and Elina had sat; the fireplace glowed with soft ambers, but once again Benjamin felt icy fingers surround his heart. And then he heard...

"Elina is gone. It has been a year since the ship bringing Kylan and Elina home from Oslo burned."

The words destroyed Benjamin's ability to breathe; he struggled for breath and words, "No, it can't be. We planned on marrying. Oh God, it can't be."

"I wish it wasn't. The old man mumbled and sat as if the grief of losing his only children on his beloved boat had killed any living spirit within him.

And Benjamin facing heartbreak, another loss, sat frozen in his grief.

Chapter Seven

Two years passed since learning of Elina's death and Benjamin spent his time working on the house; time numbed his pain and the boys filled parts of his broken spirit with their youthful exuberance. They had both finished school and didn't want to go on to university.

Joseph spent more and more time with the Caulfield boys and their mother, Edith, while William worked full time planting and tending the estate with his father. Northern Ireland's financial plight became acute, when the English put tariffs on exports from Ireland so they would not compete with English goods.

The emigration from Ireland had begun twenty years earlier when bad times and religious freedom became extreme and had continued to present day. In the spring of 1795, when Benjamin was 51 years old, he met with his sons and Theodore and Liam to discuss emigration to the United States. Their land could be sold to other planters; but with such bad times and also a drought in the north, they would get very little. Benjamin explained he knew a wealthy Englishman who had expressed interest in the O'Connor Estate with Sir Edward years before. If he could get him interested in the three parcels; the O'Connor Estate, his own estate and Theodore's allotment, perhaps they could gain enough money to help them get started in the new world.

Joseph dismissed the idea out of hand, "Father, you are not thinking straight, this is our land, this is our home, our roots go back generations. We can't just let the English drive us away."

"I feel that way too, son, but I also realize we are facing economical devastation if we don't act soon. What would you have us do?"

"If you had only spent more time with Edith; she is a very wealthy widow, and I know she likes you."

"Son, Edith is a fine woman but I don't feel love towards her. It wouldn't be fair to her to pursue her for her money."

"Oh come on, you aren't children, a partnership can be forged without deep, undying love for God's sake."

"Let's not dwell on something that's not going to happen. I think we should give emigration our sincere thought; many of our friends and neighbors have left Ireland over the years. I hear reports there is much good land available to whoever claims it first, raw, rich lands, with many lakes and rivers, deep forests and wealth to be had, and since the American Revolution the English no longer rule the colonies, so we could have the freedom from their oppressive rule. That would be a reason to go, if no other. What do you think Theodore?"

"I am getting too old to leave Benjamin. I have enough reserve to last me many years, and I could never leave Liam, Elizabeth and my grandsons, although I would miss you, William and Joseph more than I can say."

"Liam, would you not think of leaving?"

"No, Benjamin, my job is still secure with the Merchant Fleet and I can retire next year and have a good income for life. Elizabeth and the children like their life in Belfast and I know they wouldn't want to leave it."

"I guess that leaves just William and me who would even consider relocating. Are you sure, Joseph, that you would want to stay here by yourself?"

"I would rather stay close to the Caulfield's on my own, than go with you and William. I'm sorry if that hurts your feelings, but Rory, Calvin and I have plans for our future."

"What plans, my son?"

"Edith is going to put up money for us to start a delivery business in Belfast; she thinks it is a good idea."

Benjamin felt all of his 51 years; it seemed all he had worked for, all he had loved, had simply disappeared. His heart could not find joy in the land; he did not feel at home any place and his restlessness became acute. One early morning, before anyone had awoke; he went to the stable, saddled Lightening, who in his 20's, still pranced with youthfulness, and rode eastward. He left a note for William telling him he would be staying in Belfast for a few days. He didn't say he wanted to see the gentlemen who had expressed an interest in his parent's estate and while he was in Belfast he would check on ships schedules to America.

He arrived at the Clark estate outside of Belfast around mid-day and after turning Lightening over to the stable hand, approached the imposing entrance to the large mansion. After being greeted by the butler, who dispelled him of his overcoat and hat, he waited in the elaborately furnished library to the left of the entry. "Mr. McLain, how nice to see you, I've so missed your father over these last years. Thank God those hoodlums hung for their misdeeds." Sir Rodney Clark had aged; although he had been younger than Benjamin's father, it still amazed Benjamin to find him older, although he laughed at his surprise for the mirror refuted his belief that time doesn't change the appearance.

"Yes, finally the English did a good deed for our family." Benjamin said, smiling so as not to seem bitter knowing Sir Rodney, being Scottish, still became knighted for his high deeds in the English service.

"I understand they are making life very miserable for North Ireland planters and farmers. I can't see why they don't realize the damage they will do if they bankrupt Ireland. They have never had a decent policy in their relationship to Ireland. I find it hideous."

"That is partly why I'm here. I remember at one time you expressed an interest in purchasing my family's estate, and I wondered if you would still have that interest."

"I can't believe you could let it go, son, is it because of finances or other reasons?"

"It is a little of both, Sir. Since my wife and my parents are gone, there is very little meaning for me there now and since no matter how I plan and work our production, now with all the new taxes, I can't pay for the cost of the planting. I've money from my family's estate, but it is just being spent with no return."

"If you really want to sell, I'm sure we can reach a price that would be fair to both of us. I'll have an offer ready for you within the week."

"That's good Sir, because I plan on being in town for a few days and I will stop by here on my way back home." With handshake and a warm pat on his shoulder, Benjamin left the mansion, retrieved Lightening and rode off towards the port of Belfast.

After Benjamin and Sir Rodney signed their agreement of sale, Benjamin spent the spring transferring some of the portraits and antiques from the mansion to his own home and explaining to Joseph that although he and William would be going to America without him, he wanted him to have the house and land, and would give William the like amount in money he had received for the sale of the estate. "I will be taking whatever we can load on the wagon, the rest is yours."

"Father, I've proposed to Margaret, and we'd love to have the house and property. The delivery business hasn't gone well, and Calvin and Rory will pay back Edith for me. I'll do everything I can to keep our estate together and productive."

"Joseph, I've full confidence that you will, and if you change your mind about going to America someday, Sir Rodney Clark has expressed interest in buying this property too."

For the next few months, as they prepared for a sailing date in early June of 1997, from Belfast to the port at Charleston, South Carolina, Benjamin took time to ride out over the green glens and woodlands where shrubs of blackthorn, holly and honeysuckle perfumed the air, and upon reaching the seacoast, where aged cliffs pushed back against the rough waters of the northern Atlantic, he returned to the small secluded cove where he and Anna had spent time together so long ago. He found his way down the rocky path and sat quietly, listening to the songs of seabirds, remembering days past; trying to place them in a peaceful place in his heart, so he could carry them without pain. He knew every inch of this ancient land, he had invested time and soul here, but now he would leave and never return. Maybe someday his sons, their sons and daughters, and generations over times, would come here and find the spirits of their ancestors, in the beauty of Northern Ireland.

It took two days, with a wagon full of goods, for Benjamin and William to reach Belfast. Upon their arrival Liam would accompany them to the port and Joseph would ride in to get the wagon later. "You certainly look like two very weary and worn travelers."

"That isn't half of it. We slept near the wagon to protect it, and ate and slept around a fire pit we dug into the ground. William, thank God, is good at this sort of thing; I hopelessly watched on and devoured the hares he shot for our meals."

Liam laughed, "That is a site I'd like to see. I know Joseph felt bad to see you leave. I can't imagine you going so far away, but guess I can't change your mind at this point."

"No, we are on our way. We stopped by to say goodbye to Theodore. Joseph rode along side with Lightening and we left them standing together waving goodbye. It seemed my dear companion of so many years, said goodbye with his kind eyes, as I rubbed his soft nose for the last time. He is getting old, like me. I told Joseph to let him retire to pasture with a few mares to keep him company."

The ship looked heavy and strong to Benjamin, and he thought how long it had been since he first went to sea as a junior officer in the British navy; he felt at home somehow. With shipments of goods loaded, passengers boarded; the poor and less privileged on the lower decks, Benjamin and William on the upper deck with the more fortunate, the parting whistle blew and they slowly pulled away from the dock. After they found their stateroom, unpacked their bags, William said, "Well father, how about finding a place to grab a strong drink."

Benjamin smiled at his son, now twenty-five years old, wise for his years and handsome like his father, Benjamin thought, laughing to himself. "I'll go for that and let's make it a double."

The days passed by; the wind filled the sails and they made good progress, Benjamin filled a journal with all the information he received from other shipmates, many which had relatives or friends who lived in the colonies and many claimed Scots-Irish heritage; originally from Scotland and then displaced to Northern Ireland, or what they called Ulster, from the early 1600's to present. Although this ship would land in the Carolina's, others had gone further north, many landing in Pennsylvania, Boston, Massachusetts and Delaware, though rumors of late said the central plains and river valleys of South Carolina offered more opportunity, and many townships offered acreage and provisions for those who would clear and build on the land.

"Are you Benjamin McLean?" a man approaching him said.

"Yes, I am."

"My name is John Sweet, I'm returning to South Carolina in an attempt to sell the property I bought twenty years ago. Since then I've lost two sons in the America's War of Independence and I'm of an age where I plan to move on to other pursuits. I heard say you would be looking for property on your arrival to America, and I wanted to visit with you about my place. I've a map and pertinent details; would you be interested?"

They sat together, maps spread out before them, at a long table lighted by lanterns filled with whale oil, swinging loosely with the motion of the ship. "It looks like your place is in a river valley. I've heard it has been settled earlier and is not as isolated as the foothills and forests and probably safer from Indian raids too, I would think."

"All of the above. It has been producing rice in the areas close to the river and further inland we raise cattle and cotton. Soon, with the invention of the cotton gin, cotton will be the future of the Carolinas. The house is a double-Georgian, beautiful in design and construction, with landscaped gardens leading to the river, where a boat dock houses a specially constructed day-sailor for your enjoyment; many out buildings, fences, and an artesian spring furnishes unlimited amounts of fresh, pure water. The township has a small village and church. I've twenty slaves that will be sold with the property, all loyal and hardworking and they've their own furnished houses and church. There's also labor available from the poor immigrants arriving every day, if you, as many Scots-Irish, want to free your slaves."

"Let's meet up at the Inn on Broad Street for breakfast, say two days after arrival." Mr. Sweet agreed and they parted. The description and price of this southern plantation excited Benjamin. He liked the idea of managing a large estate again. He thanked the gentleman and went to find William, who had spent his days squiring a lovely young lady around the decks, with her attendant in close proximity. He found them leaning against the rail at mid-ship. "William, that's taking a chance with this young lady; what if a big wind suddenly caught the sails and the ship tipped."

"Oh, we just stopped here for a minute. Isabella, this is my father, Benjamin McLain."

They greeted and soon the young couple wandered off and Benjamin found the pub and ordered a pint. He felt proud of his sons; handsome, William darker with his Scot side showing, and Joseph, so very Irish like Lady Katherine; and yet both seemed free from pretentions about their good looks or position in life. He hoped Joseph and Margaret found happiness together and he also trusted they might join them someday in the future. He thought about the map he had been shown, and wondered if this would be their new home. He knew he had many good years ahead; he could still manage a property, ride a horse, become active in a community, but he would let William make the decision about where they lived; his future would be the priority from now on.

It took nine weeks to cross the Atlantic, and, unbelievably, the seas remained calm with just enough wind to make sailing comfortable, except the two days of rough seas that came just before their arrival at Charleston Harbor; so everyone struggled with sea legs as they disembarked. The dock, massed with passengers and workmen seemed a strange world, but Benjamin and William made their way to a livery stable and rented a carriage. They would come back to the dock in the morning to arrange for transportation of their goods.

They found the lovely inn on Broad Street where the perfume of magnolias and azaleas filled the air, moss draped oaks and tall palmetto trees shaded the lovely Georgian architecture and the quaint cobblestone streets and sidewalks added to the charm and ambience of this southern town. Benjamin breathed in all the smells; salt, sea, breeze, perfume, dust, horses; everything around him, and he knew, for the first time, he had made the right decision in coming to America.

As he sat on a lovely terrace overlooking the harbor in this spring of 1997, he let his memories flow back in time; when he sat in the big chair, little boy legs not reaching the floor, and his beautiful mother standing there scolding him and yet at the same time showing her strong love for him on her far from stern face, he realized how he had adored her and she would be in his heart forever; and then he sat with Anna in their special cove, holding and kissing with the passion of young lovers with all their life ahead of them, lovely Anna, the mother of his sons and his wife for eternity; and then without any guilt, his thoughts came to Elina, the young girl in the flowing dress, with the contagious laugh and spirited ways, to the Elina at thirty-seven, a lady with graceful composure, without losing any of that earlier spirit and beauty; his remembering their days and nights together in Belfast, brought life to his body now as he thought about her again.

At 53 years of age, Benjamin had reached a place in his life where past, present and future could be combined without regret. His time left would be spent insuring his sons had all the opportunities and independence needed to end their days in peaceful acceptance of what is and what can be.

Land Above

By Leigh Clarke

Ms. Clarke's book, *Land Above*, is a fictional story about the first generation of her family arriving in Charleston, South Carolina from Northern Ireland in 1797. The story covers the troubles between the landed Irish and the immigrant Protestants so deeply felt on a personal level by Benjamin, whose Irish mother was of landed nobility and his Protestant father an Admiral in the British Navy. Always squeezed between their desires for him, he strongly charts his own course with relationships not approved by his mother, enlistment in the Royal Navy, shipwreck, love and lost loves and finally leaving his country and landing in a new and strange land.